Oh, the Places You'll Go!

Oh, the Places You'll Go!

By Dr. Seuss

RANDOM HOUSE NEW YORK

Library of Congress Cataloging-in-Publication Data:
Seuss, Dr. Oh, the places you'll go! SUMMARY: Advice in rhyme for proceeding in life; weathering fear, loneliness, and confusion; and being in charge of your actions.   ISBN: 0-679-80527-3 (trade); 0-679-90527-8 (lib. bdg.)   [1. Success—Fiction. 2. Stories in rhyme]   I. Title.   PZ8.3.G2760g 1990   [E]   89-36892

Manufactured in Mexico   1 2 3 4 5 6 7 8 9 0

Congratulations!
Today is your day.
You're off to Great Places!
You're off and away!

You have brains in your head.
You have feet in your shoes.
You can steer yourself
any direction you choose.
You're on your own. And you know what you know.
And *YOU* are the guy who'll decide where to go.

You'll look up and down streets. Look 'em over with care.
About some you will say, "I don't choose to go there."
With your head full of brains and your shoes full of feet,
you're too smart to go down any not-so-good street.

And you may not find *any*
you'll want to go down.
In that case, of course,
you'll head straight out of town.

And you may not find *any*
you'll want to go down.
In that case, of course,
you'll head straight out of town.

It's opener there
in the wide open air.

Out there things can happen
and frequently do
to people as brainy
and footsy as you.

It's opener there
in the wide open air.

Out there things can happen
and frequently do
to people as brainy
and footsy as you.

And when things start to happen,
don't worry. Don't stew.
Just go right along.
You'll start happening too.

OH!
THE PLACES YOU'LL GO!

You'll be on your way up!
You'll be seeing great sights!
You'll join the high fliers
who soar to high heights.

You won't lag behind, because you'll have the speed.
You'll pass the whole gang and you'll soon take the lead.
Wherever you fly, you'll be best of the best.
Wherever you go, you will top all the rest.

Except when you *don't*.
Because, sometimes, you *won't*.

I'm sorry to say so
but, sadly, it's true
that Bang-ups
and Hang-ups
can happen to you.

You can get all hung up
in a prickle-ly perch.
And your gang will fly on.
You'll be left in a Lurch.

You'll come down from the Lurch
with an unpleasant bump.
And the chances are, then,
that you'll be in a Slump.

I'm sorry to say so
but, sadly, it's true
that Bang-ups
and Hang-ups
can happen to you.

You can get all hung up
in a prickle-ly perch.
And your gang will fly on.
You'll be left in a Lurch.

You'll come down from the Lurch
with an unpleasant bump.
And the chances are, then,
that you'll be in a Slump.

And when you're in a Slump,
you're not in for much fun.
Un-slumping yourself
is not easily done.

You will come to a place where the streets are not marked.
Some windows are lighted. But mostly they're darked.
A place you could sprain both your elbow and chin!
Do you dare to stay out? Do you dare to go in?
How much can you lose? How much can you win?

And *IF* you go in, should you turn left or right...
or right-and-three-quarters? Or, maybe, not quite?
Or go around back and sneak in from behind?
Simple it's not, I'm afraid you will find,
for a mind-maker-upper to make up his mind.

You can get so confused
that you'll start in to race
down long wiggled roads at a break-necking pace
and grind on for miles across weirdish wild space,
headed, I fear, toward a most useless place.

The Waiting Place...

...for people just waiting.
    Waiting for a train to go
    or a bus to come, or a plane to go
    or the mail to come, or the rain to go
    or the phone to ring, or the snow to snow
    or waiting around for a Yes or No
    or waiting for their hair to grow.
    Everyone is just waiting.

Waiting for the fish to bite
or waiting for wind to fly a kite
or waiting around for Friday night
or waiting, perhaps, for their Uncle Jake
or a pot to boil, or a Better Break
or a string of pearls, or a pair of pants
or a wig with curls, or Another Chance.
Everyone is just waiting.

NO!
That's not for you!

Somehow you'll escape
all that waiting and staying.
You'll find the bright places
where Boom Bands are playing.

With banner flip-flapping,
once more you'll ride high!
Ready for anything under the sky.
Ready because you're that kind of a guy!

Oh, the places you'll go! There is fun to be done!
There are points to be scored. There are games to be won.
And the magical things you can do with that ball
will make you the winning-est winner of all.
Fame! You'll be famous as famous can be,
with the whole wide world watching you win on TV.

Except when they don't.
Because, sometimes, they won't.

I'm afraid that *some* times
you'll play lonely games too.
Games you can't win
'cause you'll play against you.

All Alone!
Whether you like it or not,
Alone will be something
you'll be quite a lot.

And when you're alone, there's a very good chance
you'll meet things that scare you right out of your pants.
There are some, down the road between hither and yon,
that can scare you so much you won't want to go on.

But on you will go
though the weather be foul.
On you will go
though your enemies prowl.
On you will go
though the Hakken-Kraks howl.
Onward up many
a frightening creek,
though your arms may get sore
and your sneakers may leak.

On and on you will hike.
And I know you'll hike far
and face up to your problems
whatever they are.

You'll get mixed up, of course,
as you already know.
You'll get mixed up
with many strange birds as you go.
So be sure when you step.
Step with care and great tact
and remember that Life's
a Great Balancing Act.
Just never forget to be dexterous and deft.
And *never* mix up your right foot with your left.

And will you succeed?
Yes! You will, indeed!
(98 and ¾ percent guaranteed.)

KID, YOU'LL MOVE MOUNTAINS!

So...
be your name Buxbaum or Bixby or **Bray**
or Mordecai Ali Van Allen O'Shea,
you're off to Great Places!
Today is your day!
Your mountain is waiting.
So... *get on your way!*